SUPER SUSAN

MEGAN STINE & H. WILLIAM STINE

This book is dedicated to Bob and Jane
Illustrations by Dick Bangham

Copyright © 1989, 1979 by Megan Stine and H. William Stine.
All rights reserved. Published by Scholastic Inc.
SPRINT and SPRINT BOOKS are trademarks of Scholastic Inc.
Printed in the U.S.A.
ISBN 0-590-35189-3

11 12 13 14 15   23   05 04 03 02

CHAPTER 1

The woman on the airport PA was calling Susan's flight.

"Flight Number Two to New Orleans, Denver, and Japan, is now boarding at Gate Number . . ."

Susan couldn't hear the number. She was still getting an earful of instructions from her mother.

"Mom, I have to go," Susan said. "The plane is loading, and I don't know where it is! What if I get on the wrong plane? I think she said Gate Twelve."

"Well, dear, you be careful. Do everything you planned to do, but write me three times a day. Have a wonderful time, darling, but don't go out of the house if you can help it."

Susan was in a big hurry. She hugged her mom good-bye and ran to find her gate.

"Is this the plane to Denver?" she asked the man at Gate 12. But he was too busy to answer. He just took Susan's ticket and waved her on board.

"This is the most ridiculous thing I ever heard," said a woman with a parrot on her shoulder. "Why can't I take my parrot on the

plane?" she wanted to know.

"Fat chance! Fat chance!" said the parrot.

The woman on the PA began to announce again. "Last call for Flight Number Two, now boarding at —"

This time Susan couldn't hear the number because of the woman and her parrot. "My parrot won't eat much," she said. "And he wants to see the in-flight movie. I promised him."

"Lady, he'll have to wait to see it on TV," said the man behind the counter.

"Fat chance! Fat chance!" said the parrot.

Susan got on the plane.

It was crowded. Everyone looked at her strangely as she went to her seat. She wanted to ask someone if this was the right plane, but nobody was talking to anybody else. Susan sat down and buckled her seat belt. In a minute the engines roared, and Susan was pressed to the back of her chair.

After a while the seat belt sign went out. Was she on the right plane? Susan looked for a steward or stewardess. But no one was around.

Suddenly one of the passengers stood up. He turned and faced all the others in the plane.

"This is it!" he said. "We've done it! We got away and nobody saw us."

Suddenly there was a huge noise. The man standing in front said the magic word REPUS, which is SUPER backwards. A great gust of smoke went up. When it cleared, the Silver Hurricane was standing in the front of the plane. He was wearing his bright silver cape. Susan's mouth almost fell to her lap.

After that the passengers started saying magic words and doing secret handshakes. Some of them were rubbing magic rings. Soon the plane was filled with every superhero Susan had read about and seen on TV. The Flyman was there. He had big eyes that could see four ways at one time. And there was

Hungryman, who had eaten his way through cities and into the hearts of millions. Over there was the Blue Flash, the fastest person in the world. Susan also saw Allergyman, whose sneeze could knock over a building. And there was the Indescribable Yecch, who was the ugliest and most disgusting thing that ever fought for goodness and truth.

Susan couldn't believe her eyes. They were all there, and their clothes were even brighter in real life. Susan was on the wrong plane. That was for sure!

Someone hung a huge banner across the front of the plane. It said: THE SUPERHEROES' FIRST ANNUAL SUMMER VACATION. Everyone cheered when the sign went up.

Then, one by one, everyone turned to look at Susan. The Silver Hurricane came down to where she sat.

"I'm the Silver Hurricane, the Power of the Wind," he said. "Who are you?"

Susan said, "Uh, I'm Susan . . . from Fort Wayne, Indiana."

"Susan from Fort Wayne?" said a woman in a red and purple cape. "I've never heard of Susan. Are you sure you're one of us?"

"Oh, take it easy, Worrywoman," said Allergyman, putting a tissue up to his sore nose. "This must be Super Susan. The amazing

10

ten-year-old girl."

"I'm not a superhero," Susan said. "I'm just a normal girl."

But Worrywoman interrupted her. "Why aren't you wearing your uniform?" she asked.

"I don't have one, that's why. You see, this is all a big mistake. I was just going on vacation to see —"

The Silver Hurricane spoke up. "Of course, you're going on vacation. We're all on vacation, aren't we, cousin crime-fighters?"

The superheroes jumped up and cheered again.

"Three full weeks of swimming and sunning with nobody bothering us to catch a bank robber or save the world," said Allergyman.

"When do we eat?" asked Hungryman.

"That's a good question," said the Silver Hurricane. "But you've been asking us that since breakfast! Super Susan, I welcome you!"

"Thank you," Susan said. "Is this plane going to Denver?"

"Denver?" laughed the Silver Hurricane. All the people on the plane laughed. "We're going to a secret destination. A hide-out that only two people know about — the plane's captain and me."

Suddenly Susan wasn't hungry. Would she ever see her Aunt Edna and Uncle Burt in Denver? How would she get back home to Fort Wayne, Indiana? What if these superheroes expected her to fly with the rest of them? Susan wasn't hungry at all.

"Attention, passengers," said a voice on the intercom. "This is your captain speaking. I'd like to welcome you to this secret flight. Our expected arrival time is two hours from now. Please sit back and enjoy your flight. Oh, yes, one more thing. I've been informed there is a horrible, fiendish villain on the plane. Have a happy flight."

Then he signed off.

CHAPTER 2

A villain on the plane! Nobody would believe it. The world's greatest superheroes looked at each other. One of them was a horrible, fiendish villain. They had to find out who!

"I knew something would ruin our vacation," Worrywoman said. "It never fails."

"Yeah," said everyone else.

"I'll prove I'm the real Allergyman. I'll sneeze."

"No, don't do that," said Worrywoman. "You'll blast a hole in the plane, and we'll crash. We've got to find this villain, and we've got to find him fast."

"How do we know it's a *him*?" said another superhero, looking directly at Susan. It took a lot of nerve, but Susan stared right back without moving a muscle.

I may be on the wrong plane, and I may not be Super Susan. But I'm no villain, Susan told herself.

But they kept at it. They accused each other of being the villain. Susan couldn't believe it. Superheroes were fighting each other! Only a horrible, fiendish villain could start this.

15

"Wait a minute, wait a minute," she yelled. "This isn't getting you anywhere."

Everyone stopped to hear Susan.

"There's only one way to find the villain. We have to wait until he or she does something bad."

"Well put, Super Susan," said the Silver Hurricane.

"I think Super Susan is right. Let's sit down and wait," said Hungryman. "In the meantime, let's eat lunch!"

They sat and they waited. Thirty minutes . . . forty-five minutes . . . an hour later, lunch was finally served. Everyone was super hungry. The superheroes dug into the food.

But just as Susan was taking a bite of her food, the plane shook and knocked the food into her lap.

"Look," said Allergyman. "Susan has food in her lap. She's spelling out secret words with it."

"No, she's just a sloppy eater," said the Blue Flash. The plane shook again, and food flew on all the superheroes. The plane shook again, and the food kept flying. No one could eat.

"This is the captain speaking. We've run into some rough flying. I'm sure I'll be able to steer around it, so please enjoy your meal." The plane shook worse than ever! Plates and

silverware were thrown all over the place.

A villain couldn't ask for a prettier sight, Susan thought.

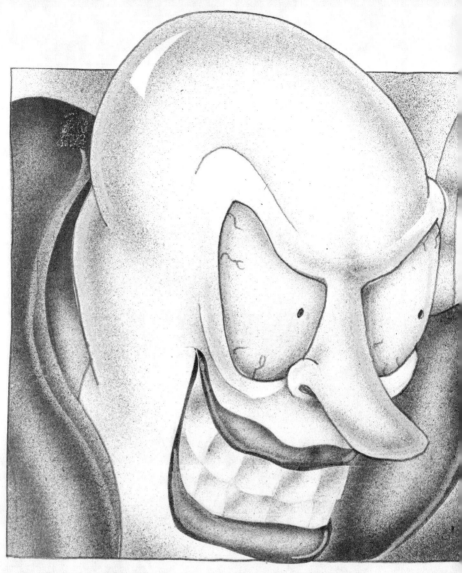

And then something clicked in her head. Of course! she thought. The villain did this! A villain loves to see superheroes fight among themselves. Only a villain would make us hungry and then ruin our meal!

Susan jumped up and ran to the front of the plane. Dodging flying food, she made it to the door of the cockpit. She listened at the door,

and then she pushed it open.

At the controls of the plane was a large man dressed completely in black. His head was round and bald. He must have heard Susan, because he turned to look at her with his red, glowing eyes. His teeth looked like mirrors.

Susan slammed the door and ran back to the others.

"I know who the villain is. It's the pilot of the plane!" she yelled above the crashing plates. But the superheroes were arguing worse than ever, and they ignored her.

"Do something to make them stop," Susan pleaded with Sunburst. Sunburst could use the light of the sun.

She began to glow yellow and then blazed red. Finally the superheroes stopped fighting because they knew Sunburst was signaling that danger was near.

"I know who the villain is," Susan said.

"Good. Tell us who," said Confused Man. "I hope it's not me."

"It's none of you," Susan said. "It's the pilot. I just saw him."

"Great work," said Worrywoman. "I always knew you were one of us. Come on, everyone. Let's get him!"

They rushed to the cockpit and Muscleman knocked the door down with his little finger. But there was no pilot! There was no villain. He was gone.

"He was sitting right here," Susan said.

"He must have bailed out," said Allergyman.

"Did you get a good look at him?" the Silver Hurricane asked.

"A better look than I wanted to get!" Susan said.

21

"Did he have red eyes and a bald head?" asked the Silver Hurricane.

"Did he look like a cantaloupe with eyes?" asked Hungryman.

Susan nodded, surprised.

"Look. He left a note pinned to the captain's chair," she said.

"I'll bet it's not good news," said Worrywoman.

The Silver Hurricane blew the letter out of the envelope. Then he read the note:

Dear Super-suckers,

You win this round. But this is only the beginning of my plot. Soon you will find out how I plan to ruin your vacations. I'll make you wretched for the whole three weeks. You'll never swim, you'll never get a tan. You'll never play volleyball. And you'll never get a minute's rest—not while I'm around. And on top of that, I'm destroying the Earth. Give up. Your efforts are wasted.

Until next we meet,
Krazlo

P.S. To the one you call Super Susan: Watch your step! I'll get you if you come snooping around again. I don't forget!

CHAPTER 3

Suddenly Susan was sitting down. She hadn't planned to sit down, but after reading Krazlo's note, her legs gave out. She wondered why she had ever wanted to leave Fort Wayne.

"Sounds as if you've been put at the top of Krazlo's most-hated list," said Worrywoman.

"Fear not, Super Susan," said the Silver Hurricane. "We have defeated him before, and we will defeat him again."

"We may have defeated him, but we've never been able to catch him," said Allergyman.

"That's true," said the Hurricane. "He is the cruelest and most heartless of all the villains we've battled. He's caused wars between planets. I remember when he burned the planet Zolor to a crisp."

"Yeah," said Worrywoman. "It was terrible. Worse than that, he's the man who invented scraping fingernails across a blackboard."

That sent a chill down Susan's back.

"Last year he tried to blow up a dam and flood the Earth," said Sunburst.

"Oh, no," Susan said. Krazlo was definitely the worst villain around.

"Yes," said Allergyman. "And for my birthday last year, he sent me a turtleneck sweater with the turtle still in it."

"Now he's going to destroy the Earth," the Silver Hurricane said. "We have to discover Krazlo's plot."

"Let's sit down and clear our heads for a minute," said Worrywoman.

"That's a good idea. Does anyone want to use my nose spray? It really clears my head fast," said Allergyman.

"That's not what I meant," Worrywoman said. "I meant that we should come up with a good plan."

"Aren't you forgetting something important?" Susan said. "Who's flying this plane?"

"We're going to crash! I should have known it," said Worrywoman.

"Don't panic," said the Blue Flash. "We'll just jump out of the plane and fly to our hotel."

"Oh, no! I can't do that," Susan said before she could stop herself. Susan couldn't fly.

"Why not?" someone asked.

"I, uh . . . well, what about my suitcase? It's brand new. It'll be ruined in the crash."

"But you can buy a new suitcase later," said Worrywoman.

"But I like this suitcase," Susan insisted. She knew it was a flimsy excuse.

"Well, OK," said Allergyman. "Does anyone know how to fly this plane?"

A small sound came from the middle of the crowd. It sounded like someone speaking, but no one could hear what was being said.

"Did someone say something?" asked Susan. She pointed to a little man in the crowd. "Speak up, you don't have to be shy."

"Yes, he does," said Worrywoman. "He's Shyman."

The little man's face turned red. "I was, well, I mean, that is — I don't want to be any trouble, but — oh, you don't want to hear me . . ."

"Shyman, we don't have much time. Do you or don't you know how to fly a plane?" asked Worrywoman.

Susan held her breath.

"Well, you might say that. Yes, I do."

"Why didn't you say so in the first place?" said Worrywoman. "Get up here and take over."

"Well, if nobody minds," said the little man. He sat down in the pilot's seat and put on the headphones. Then he said in his biggest voice, "OK, clear the decks. I'm bringing this baby in!"

When the plane landed, Susan wanted to kiss the ground. But she didn't. Instead she ran to the nearest telephone booth to call her aunt Edna and Uncle Burt.

But the phone was out of order. In another hour the plane would land in Denver — the plane she was *supposed* to be on. Aunt Edna and Uncle Burt would notice that she wasn't on it. Then what would they do?

"Super Susan, you don't have to use a telephone. Just call out in your super voice," said the Silver Hurricane.

"I can't," Susan said. "Because, uh, because I wanted to make it person-to-person."

"Welcome to the Harry Arms Hotel," said the desk clerk. He didn't smile, and he sounded

like a robot. "How may I assist you?"

"We'd like the keys to our rooms," said the Silver Hurricane.

"Your name?" asked the desk clerk.

"Don't you recognize me?" Hurricane said. "I'm the Silver Hurricane!"

"I'm sorry, Mr. Hurricane, but I don't see any

reservations in your name," said the desk clerk. He stared straight ahead.

"But you didn't look in your book," said Allergyman.

"I'd never forget a name like 'Mr. Hurricane.'"

"I don't know what's going on, but I'm beginning to get angry," said the Silver Hurricane. "We made reservations a month ago. We want fifty rooms. We're on vacation!"

"Too bad. You don't have reservations and I don't have any rooms. You'll have to leave now. We don't allow people to hang around our lobby."

"Listen, maybe you don't know who you're talking to," Susan said, getting angry too.

"How could I miss it?" the desk clerk said. "They have their names written all over their shirts!"

Susan slipped off to use the pay phone. She put a dime in it, but the phone was still dead. So were the others next to it.

"Is your desk phone working?" Susan asked the clerk.

"No. We must be having trouble with the line," he told Susan. But he hadn't even picked up the phone to check.

That was when Susan noticed that the desk clerk's eyes looked a little red.

By the time she got outside to meet the others, the adding machine in her head was putting two and two together again.

"What's the first thing a villain does when he gets to town?" Susan asked the crowd.

"He usually cuts the phone lines," said Worrywoman. "I've seen it on TV."

"Well, the phones in this town are dead, and the desk clerk looks like he's half dead too," Susan said. "I don't know what we're going to do, but I know that Krazlo is very near. I don't know how he got here so fast. And I don't know what he's going to do next. But I'm sure of one thing: He's right here in this very hotel. And he's going to get *me*!"

CHAPTER 4

"If Krazlo is here, we're going to need all our strength," said Worrywoman. "We'd better get something to eat." She led the group into the hotel snack shop. "Let's all be sure to get a well-balanced meal."

"What'll it be?" asked the waitress.

"I'd like a hamburger with a pickle." Susan said.

"Not healthy enough," said Worrywoman. "We have to fight the worst villain in the universe."

"In that case," said Susan, "I'll have a *cheese*burger with a pickle."

The waitress called her order to the cook in special waitress language. "Grease the tubes!" she shouted. She turned to the Silver Hurricane and said, "What do you want?"

"I'd like a steak with french fries and green beans," he said.

"Make it two!" called the waitress. Then she turned to the Indescribable Yecch. "What do you want? A glass of water to wash off your face?"

"I don't suppose you have glorbis. It's a very

popular dish on my planet," said the Yecch.

"Sure we do," she said. "Grease the tubes!"
she called out again.

No matter what anyone ordered, the waitress
called the same thing to the cook. Something
was going on, and Susan began to look for
clues.

The food came, and everyone got up to step
away from it. Whatever it was, it was mostly
gray with green flecks.

"I don't know whether to eat it or fight it,"
said Muscleman.

"Is there something wrong with the food?" the waitress asked in a dead voice.

"Look," said the Silver Hurricane. "Her eyes are red!"

"Maybe she ate some of this food," said Allergyman.

"No," said Susan. "Krazlo has her under his power, just like the desk clerk. Krazlo must be somewhere near."

"We'd better start saving our energy," said Worrywoman. "Super Susan and I will look around. The rest of you stay here."

When Susan and Worrywoman returned, the crowd let out a roar. Susan thought they were cheering, but then she realized it was their stomachs growling.

"Well, everybody," Susan began, "we've been all over town."

"And we have some terrible, terrible, news." said Worrywoman.

"First of all, we checked the hotel gift shop," said Susan. "There's no suntan oil, no sunglasses, no beach rafts, and no rubber balls."

"Oh, no!" everyone said at once. "What are we going to do?"

"Second of all," Susan said, "there's very little sun in the sky. In fact every second it gets darker and darker. I hate to tell you this, but I think Krazlo is putting out the sun."

Everyone was silent. The superheroes knew this would destroy the Earth once and for all.

"Hot dogs! Get your red hots right here!" called a man outside.

Everyone turned. At first they thought they were seeing things. But it was real. The food was real. A little man in a funny hat and black sunglasses stood there. He pushed a hot dog cart.

"Get 'em while they're hot! Hot dogs," he called.

There was a scramble and a cloud of dust. All the superheroes were still very hungry. Hungryman was first in line, of course.

"One with mustard," he said to the old man. "And one with relish and one with ketchup and one with —"

"Only one to a customer," the man said. He handed Hungryman the hot dog.

"You're going to eat that?" Worrywoman asked Hungryman.

"I'm not going to dance on it," Hungryman said.

"Do you know what's in a hot dog? It's not good for you. What you need are vitamins, not junk like that," Worrywoman said.

"What I need is more eating and less talking," Hungryman said, opening his mouth wide.

Susan watched the little old man go away. "Wait a minute! Don't eat that!" she said. "You forgot the mustard." She walked over to the old man's cart.

"Mustard, please," she said to him.

As the old man bent over to find the mustard, his sunglasses slipped. For a split-second Susan saw the glare of bright red eyes. With a sweep of her arm, she knocked the old man's hat off. A shining bald head was underneath.

"It's Krazlo!" Susan screamed, running away.

Krazlo watched her. Then he threw the hot dog after her. In an instant, Hungryman flew through the air toward the hot dog. He caught it in his open mouth and swallowed. But the force of it threw him spinning to the ground. When the dust cleared and Hungryman stood up, they saw Krazlo had escaped.

"Does anyone have something for a terrible case of heartburn?" asked Hungryman, shaking the dirt off.

But Susan was looking toward the sun again. The sky was turning very black.

"He's doing it," she said. "Krazlo is putting out the sun. We've got to think of a plan, and fast!"

"If he puts out the sun, my allergies will never dry up," said Allergyman.

"Your allergies?" snapped Leadingman, the superhero from Hollywood. "What about my beautiful tan? If he puts out the sun, I won't be able to make any more movies."

"Without the sun, I won't have powers at all," said Sunburst. "I'm getting weak already."

"What are we going to do?" Susan asked.

"We'll do what we've always done," cried the Silver Hurricane. "We'll beat Krazlo at his own game!"

39

CHAPTER 5

"We'd like to use the hotel dining room to hold a meeting," Susan said to the desk clerk. His eyes weren't red anymore. But his temper wasn't any better.

"Only guests of the hotel may use the dining room," he said. "That's the rule. And since you have no rooms here, you aren't guests of the hotel. And don't forget the rule about hanging around the lobby."

"Listen, you," Susan said angrily. "Your phones are dead, your food is rotten, and your gift shop is empty. This is a terrible place. If you don't do what we say, we're going to write mean letters about you. No one will ever come here again. What do you think about that?"

"'Wait until I turn on the air conditioning in the dining room," said the man. "I want you to be comfortable." He hurried to show them the way.

"Are we all here?" asked Worrywoman, counting heads. It was a difficult thing to do when she came to the Indescribable Yecch. "Someone is missing. Where is the Silver Hurricane?"

"I don't know. I haven't seen him since we

41

came inside," the Blue Flash said, sounding worried.

Just then the big wooden doors of the dining room burst open. A silver swirl of wind swept into the room. It was the Silver Hurricane.

"Where have you been?" they asked.

The Silver Hurricane looked miserable. "To the sun," he said. "I flew to the sun to see if I could blow the clouds away. But I failed completely."

It was getting darker outside. Susan had to think of a plan. "Well, that just means this is a job for everyone," Susan said. "I'll bet if we all joined together, we could do something."

"Susan is right," everyone cheered.

"Super Susan is wrong!" came a loud, gruff voice from the back of the room. There in the doorway stood KRAZLO.

"First you discover me in the plane," Krazlo said. "Then you uncover my hot-dog-vendor disguise."

Krazlo was walking closer and closer to where Susan was standing.

"And now I discover that you are the leader of this super zoo! Super Susan, you will bother me no more. Look into my eyes."

Susan looked at the burning red eyes and started feeling weak. Everything went black, but that was because Allergyman threw his

42

cape over Susan's head!

"Never look into his eyes, Super Susan," cried the Silver Hurricane, stepping between Susan and Krazlo. "The fiend can make people do whatever he wants. That's how he controlled the desk clerk and the waitress."

"Move aside," Krazlo snarled. "This girl is always in my way."

"You'd have to fight me first," the Silver Hurricane said. He was already beginning to turn into the shiny swirl of wind.

Krazlo said simply, "I will fight."

Again and again with all his force the Silver Hurricane swooped down on Krazlo. Krazlo stood his ground against the winds. But finally he fell to his knees. He looked up and laughed.

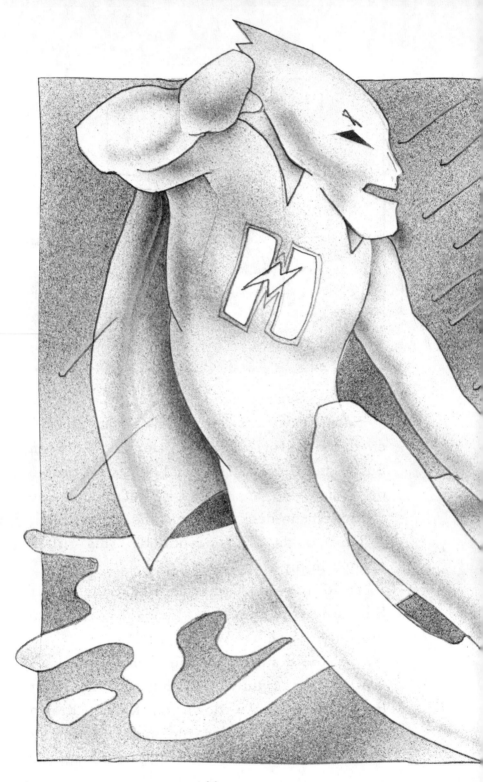

46

"Yes, go ahead. Use up all your power. Then you will be of no use to the Earth. You'll never be able to save the sun."

"He's right, Hurricane," said Allergyman. "You'd better catch your breath while I take him."

Krazlo smiled as he got up. "Do you think I'm not prepared for you, too?" Krazlo reached into the folds of his cape and threw a fistful of dust at Allergyman. "Here, have some pollen. That should fix you."

Allergyman's eyes started to tear and run. He held his finger under his nose, but it was too late. Allergyman let go a giant sneeze that sent Krazlo flying through the hotel wall. But he was back in a second.

"Who's next?" Krazlo asked, out of breath.

It was Worrywoman who stepped forward.

"You don't want to fight me, Worrywoman. You're worried that if something happens to you, no one will be able to protect Super Susan. And you're worried that if you can beat me, you won't be able to think of the right plan to save the Earth. And you're worried about what I'm going to do with the others. You're so busy worrying that you really don't want to fight me."

But Krazlo didn't know that Worrywoman never worried when she had to fight. And right then she was thinking about what she would do.

"Well, I've decided what to do," Worrywoman said. She pulled Krazlo's hat down over his face. "When in doubt, punt," she said. Then she tossed the villain to Muscleman, who kicked Krazlo out of the dining room.

"Three points," said Worrywoman.

"You haven't seen the last of me, Super Susan," Krazlo shrieked in the distance.

The room looked like a war had taken place in it. Tables and chairs were scattered and broken everywhere. There were two big holes in the wall, each one the size of Krazlo.

"The sun is half covered. That means somewhere in the world it's starting to get cold. Look at poor Sunburst. She's only as

bright as a flashlight now. Are we going to let a few bumps and bruises stop us?"

The Silver Hurricane knew the answer. They all knew the answer. They stood up and joined hands to strengthen themselves.

"You're all wonderful," Susan said. "You did this to save me. Thank you all. But could I ask one tiny favor? Could somebody take this cape off my head? I can't see a thing!"

CHAPTER 6

Susan walked back and forth across the dining room. Occasionally she stepped over a sleeping superhero.

"OK, Super Susan," she said to herself. "You're so great at coming up with plans. Let's see you come up with your best one yet. At school when the kids want to plan a surprise party, they come to you. You think of a way to keep the person from finding out about the surprise. Well, this is another kind of surprise party."

She stopped and looked out the window. The sun was almost completely covered in clouds. Susan started walking through the hotel. It was empty now, except for the superheroes sleeping to recover their strength. A news bulletin came on the television set in the lobby.

"This is Brad Bushwick in the Channel 7 newsroom. Freezing temperatures in June are causing tragedies all over America. A record 350 feet of snow fell on Rhode Island today, and the small state sank into the Atlantic Ocean.

"Freezing temperatures also struck Florida's

famous orange groves. But they're not worried there. They'll just sell it as frozen orange juice without the cans.

"And in Washington, DC, Congress has changed the national mascot from the bald eagle to the polar bear. For an explanation of all these events, I'm being joined in the studio by Doctor Noel Watson, a famous scientist."

The camera showed a man in a white doctor's coat.

"Tell me, Doctor," Brad said, "in simple terms, what is happening?"

Dr. Watson thought for a moment and said, "In simple terms, Brad, I haven't the slightest idea."

"But you're supposed to be an expert," Brad said.

"Even an expert doesn't know everything," said Dr. Watson.

"We paid you five hundred dollars to come on this show," Brad said, sweating heavily. "We already gave you the money."

"I may not know everything, but I'm not stupid. I need the money," Dr. Watson said. He stood up and left.

"So there is the scientific explanation," Brad said. "And now for the weather in our area. Let's go over to Steve O'Donnell at the weather map."

"Thanks, Brad," said Steve. "Here's the forecast, and it doesn't look too bright. Cloudy today, followed by more cloudiness tomorrow. The forecast for Sunday is very, very cloudy and cold. And for all of next week — cloudy. Now back to you, Brad."

"I've just been handed another bulletin," Brad said. "Scientists have decided that it is freezing because the sun is going out. The Earth is going to freeze solid in less than forty-eight hours. This is Brad Bushwick saying — have a good day until tomorrow."

Susan turned off the television. "It's started! The world is beginning to freeze."

"I'm so cold," said a voice. It was Sunburst.

"Can I get you a blanket?" Susan asked.

"No, I need heat and light. I need the sun," Sunburst said.

"Should I wake up the others?" Susan asked.

"No, don't do that. They haven't recovered yet. I'm sure I can hold out," Sunburst said weakly.

But Susan could see she was fading fast.

I wish I were Super Susan. I'd get Krazlo for this, Susan thought. Susan let go of Sunburst's chilly hand. I've got to think of something. Sunburst is the only one who can save the sun.

Susan saw a big black cat in the dining room. It was so big and fat, it looked as if it

54

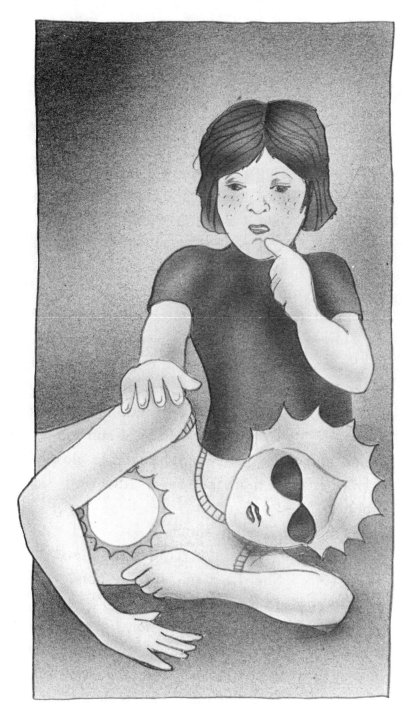

didn't have a neck. The cat was sleeping, curled up under a lamp.

"Hello, kitty cat," Susan said, petting it. The cat reminded her of Gary, her own cat at home. Gary always slept under her desk lamp because the heat from the bulb kept him warm.

"That's it! That's the answer!" Susan went running through the hotel, looking for sun lamps! They could save Sunburst. The hotel had a swimming pool with sun lamps. Susan gathered up every sun lamp she could find and took them into the dining room.

"Sunburst, you're going to be all right — if I don't blow a fuse." Susan switched on the lamps, and the light got so bright that she had to look away.

"What's going on?" some of the superheroes asked. They looked at the circle of sun lamps. Inside it, a small yellow light began to glow. It turned orange and red as it lifted off the ground.

"It's Sunburst!" they shouted.

"Follow me," Sunburst called in a strong, clear voice. She flew out of the hotel and headed straight for the sun.

"What are we waiting for, a written invitation? Follow that superhero," said the Silver Hurricane. All the superheroes took off. "Come on, Super Susan. Come with us," the

Silver Hurricane called back.

"Uh, I'll change and catch up with you in a minute," she said.

"On to the sun!" he cried, and then he was out of sight.

That was quick thinking, Susan, she told herself. They still think I'm a superhero. How am I going to tell them? Well, I may never see them again unless they can save the sun.

Susan sat down and fell asleep. But she had bad dreams. Suddenly she woke up with the feeling she wasn't alone. She turned her head slowly one way and then the other. There was the fat, black cat again. It was crying and rubbing up against a chair.

"It's probably hungry," said Susan. "So am I."

She took the cat and went exploring. The snack shop was deserted now, but there was someone in the kitchen. Susan could hear the rattling of pots and pans.

"Is anyone here?" Susan called.

No answer.

"I said, is anybody here?" she said louder.

"Yes, you and I are here — just the two of us — alone," said Krazlo, stepping out of a shadow. "I told you I never forget!"

CHAPTER 7

Susan looked away from Krazlo and started walking slowly to the door.

"There is no escape," Krazlo said with a laugh.

The fat black cat was standing by the door. Suddenly it arched its back, and its fur stood up. When Susan looked at its eyes, she could see they were bright red.

"You see," said Krazlo. "My new little friend won't let you pass . . . not in one piece."

Susan backed away from the door and looked around. There was no other way out.

"I've done it. I've finally defeated the super fools. They fell for my trick!"

"What trick?" asked Susan. "They're flying to save the sun, and then they'll be back to take care of you."

"Save the sun? That makes me laugh. Ha ha ha ha," Krazlo said. "The sun is in no danger. I knew Sunburst would blow the clouds away."

"You mean you didn't plan to destroy the Earth?" Susan asked.

"I don't want to destroy the Earth," Krazlo shouted. "I want to take over the Earth! I want to rule the planet, and have every living thing

do as I command. And that's the way it's going to be with your superhero friends out in space."

Susan carefully backed up to the counter. She had a plan all worked out. As long as Krazlo stayed behind her, she thought it might work.

"Well, look at that," Krazlo said. "Isn't that Worrywoman outside?"

Susan's heart jumped. She turned toward the window without looking up. She saw Krazlo's shoes, and then she knew immediately it was a trick to make her look at him.

"Look at me! Look at me, you little fool!" he cried.

"How about sending me a picture instead?" Susan said.

"You're too smart, Super Susan, but I'll make you look at me."

He came toward her. Her plan had to work—and it had to work now! With a quick sweep of her hand, Susan knocked the cream off the counter. It crashed to the floor and the black cat ran to drink it. Now the door was clear, and Susan ran for it. But Krazlo was after her. She was faster, but she didn't know who was going to win. As she ran past a mirror in the lobby, she couldn't help it. Something made her look in it. In the mirror

she saw two red, burning eyes. Her body felt warm, and she fell to the ground.

"I've got you," Krazlo said, throwing her into a chair. "Now, Super Susan, you will do exactly as I say. You will help me take over the world."

"Yes, I will help you," Susan said, although she didn't want to. She couldn't control herself. Her eyes were like red-hot steel.

"Good. Come with me." Krazlo led Susan out of the hotel to the parking garage. He gave his ticket to the attendant, who soon returned with Krazlo's big car. "That will be five dollars, please," said the man.

Krazlo didn't give the man any money. He looked at the man and the attendant's eyes went from brown to red.

"Thank you, sir," he said to Krazlo. "Thank you, and here is your change."

Then the man counted 200 dollars in five-dollar bills and gave it to Krazlo.

"It's going to be so easy," laughed Krazlo. "So easy."

He put Susan in the car and drove off.

Where is he taking me? Susan wondered. Wherever it is, it must be a terrible place.

Krazlo drove like a madman. Pretty soon the car was going up a steep hill. At the very top was a crumbling castle. Bats flew around it, and all the trees were dead and brown. The window curtains were torn and dirty. This must be Krazlo's castle, Susan thought.

"How can people live in that rat trap?" Krazlo said. "It's disgusting." He gunned the car and sped past the castle.

Just up the road from the castle was a small mobile home. Krazlo pulled into the driveway.

"It isn't much, but it's home," he said. He went in and got a guitar case. "This is how I'll take over the entire world. I'm going to start a rock group. I'm calling it 'the Forces of Evil.' Kids love rock groups. They buy all their albums and go to their concerts. They pay attention to all the words in the songs. They like to do whatever the stars tell them. Wait until they hear my songs. They'll do whatever I sing — I'll be able to rule the world!"

Then Krazlo began to sing one of his songs. The words went like this:

When the world's got you down
and you're feeling real sad,
don't just do *something* —
do something bad.

"Remember that song, Super Susan, because you're going to be a singer in my group. Now all I have to do is find the rest of the group."

The car roared down the road toward the city.

68

CHAPTER 8

Krazlo stopped the car. There was a large crowd waiting outside the City Auditorium. Young people lined up for two blocks. People pushed, voices squealed, and the lights blazed.

APPEARING TONIGHT!
ONE PERFORMANCE ONLY!
BARRY STARR AND THE MILKY WAY!

Dragging Susan by the arm, Krazlo pushed his way to the box office.

"Hey, look at those two. They're walking to the front of the line. Who do they think they are?" someone said.

"Maybe they're teachers," someone else answered.

"I want two tickets for tonight," Krazlo said to the woman at the box office.

"So do all these people, Baldy," said the woman. "But don't bother getting in line because we're all sold out."

Krazlo stared deeply into her eyes until they were as red as his.

"Here," the woman said. "I bought two tickets for my daughters who have been waiting a whole year to see Barry Starr. Take my two tickets."

"Thanks, I will," said Krazlo.

"That will be thirty dollars," said the woman. Krazlo stared harder at her. She said, "Thank you, sir, and here is your change. Then she counted out 200 dollars and handed it to Krazlo. He laughed and dragged Susan into the auditorium.

"Now we're going backstage. I'm sure no one will mind." He saw a sign on a door: BACKSTAGE — STAY OUT!

They opened the door and went into the band's dressing room.

"Hey, look what just walked in," snickered one of the guys, looking at Krazlo. "A bowling ball on legs."

"Boys," said Krazlo. "Pack up your guitars. You and I are forming a new band."

"Come on, man, we already work for the number-one singer in the country, Barry Starr," said Johnny Day, strumming his guitar.

"In a week Barry Starr's name will be mud," said Krazlo.

"Why? Is he having it legally changed?" Johnny Day asked.

"Never mind that. Just pack your stuff and let's go. I'll pay you a thousand dollars a minute."

"Every rock star gets that much," said the others.

"OK, I'll double it," Krazlo said.

"Why didn't you say so in the first place?" said the drummer.

"We'll take it," Johnny Day said.

"Pack your things," said Krazlo. "Let's go."

"Wait a minute. I have an important question," said Johnny Day. "Why would anyone change their name to Mud Starr?"

"I'll explain later," Krazlo sneered. "We have

71

to go rehearse now."

Susan saw the musicians' eyes turning red. Hot red.

They went back to the Harry Arms Hotel and rehearsed for hours and hours.

Krazlo's songs are bad enough. Wait until people hear his singing, Susan thought. She was still under Krazlo's power, so she stood silently in the corner.

"Who is she?" wondered the keyboard man. "She hasn't said a word the whole time we've been here."

"She's one of the singers," Krazlo answered. "You guys must be tired. We've been playing for six straight hours. Take a five-minute break, and then we'll try it again."

The four musicians fell over and immediately were sound asleep. Then Krazlo looked at Susan. "Super Susan, come here. I want you to make a telephone call."

In a few minutes Susan was calling the local radio station.

"Hello, this is WROK," said the voice. "You're calling the lighter than light, all-night radio show."

"Hello? This is Kathy," said Susan, just as Krazlo had instructed her. "Are you going to play the new record by the Forces of Evil?"

"Never heard of them," said the announcer.

"But all the kids at school say that anyone who's never heard of the Forces of Evil must be nowhere. You know, an absolute zip."

The announcer got a little nervous. "Oh, you mean the Forces of Evil," he said. "Sure, I knew who they were all the time. I was just kidding you."

"Well, there is a Forces of Evil concert tomorrow, and it's all sold out," Susan said.

Susan hung up the phone, and Krazlo turned on the radio to WROK.

"Hey there, guys and gals. Don't miss tomorrow's concert by the Forces of Evil. If you do, you're nowhere — an absolute zip. Right, Kathy?"

Krazlo laughed and laughed. "This is too easy, too easy. OK, you guys, let's run through the songs again."

But the band was asleep. Nothing could wake them up, not even 20,000 dollars a minute.

"Maybe a little nap would do some bad," Krazlo said. "I can't expect to do my evil best on no sleep." He stretched out on the couch and fell sound asleep.

The instant he fell asleep, the spell was broken. Susan's eyes turned from red to blue, and her body relaxed.

She took a deep breath. She didn't have much time. Krazlo could wake up any moment. But as usual Susan had a plan.

Quietly Susan picked up the telephone. She

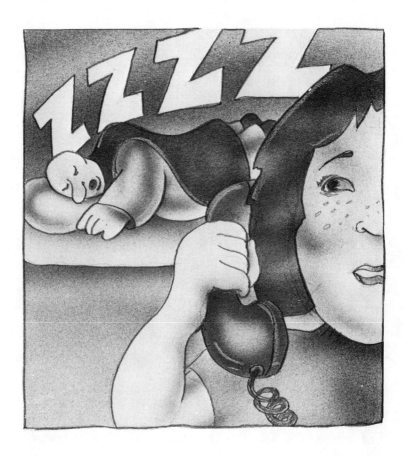

called the newspapers, the radio stations, and the TV stations. She even called *Weekly*, the national news magazine. She gave each of them the same message: Come to the hotel if you want to capture the horrible, fiendish villain, Krazlo.

This time without the superheroes — all by myself — I'm going to teach Krazlo a lesson he'll never forget, Susan thought. She hung up the phone and waited, hoping they'd get there before Krazlo woke up.

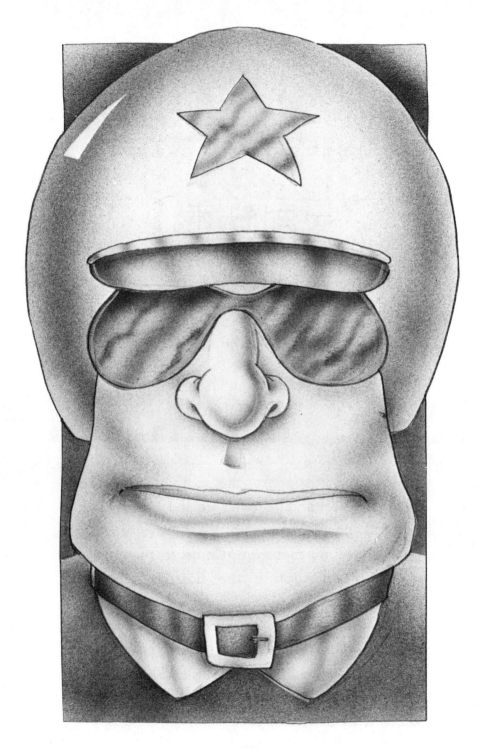

CHAPTER 9

It took half an hour for all the reporters to arrive at the hotel. They were up front with their cameras and lights. Susan had to squint to see the crowd.

A big, burly man came up to her. "Are you the girl who made those phone calls about the villain?" he asked.

Susan nodded.

"Well, I'm the Chief of Police, and my men and I are here to help you. The Riot Squad is here. And I've got my SWAT team, my SWIPE team, and my SWAK team. I've even got the swim team from the high school. We're going to get this guy."

"Tell them all to go home, Chief," Susan said. "Violence won't work.

"Listen, everybody," she called. "There's no way to fight Krazlo. I've seen how powerful he is. He can do whatever he wants. But there is a way to stop his newest plan — his plan to form a rock group and take over the world."

"Move out of the way," said the Chief of Police. "We'll get him while he's out. We'll nab him on the spot."

"No," Susan said. "I'm telling you that his

powers are too great. Now listen to me. I have a plan. Let's give Krazlo plenty of publicity and make him a huge success. We'll give him so much attention that it will drive him out of his mind. Crowds will mob him. It will be more than he can take."

"It's crazy. It'll never work," said the police chief.

"Maybe it's not so crazy," said a man with a cigar. "Yesterday I was Barry Starr's manager, and today his name is mud. The world needs a new rock star. I'll help you, kid."

"Thanks," Susan said. "Who else thinks my plan will work?"

Everyone agreed that it was worth a try. So Susan showed them the way to Krazlo's room.

"Who is it? Who is there?" asked Krazlo in a sleepy voice.

The door burst open and the reporters filled the room. They asked him questions. Photographers took his picture. TV cameramen filmed him. And radio announcers put microphones in his face. Krazlo's red eyes looked dazed.

"Tell me, Mr. Krazlo," asked a reporter. "Is it true that bad breath is one of your evil inventions?"

Flashbulbs flashed and popped.

"Mr. Krazlo, I represent the True-to-Life

Hairpiece Company. Would you sign this contract, please? It says we'll pay you two hundred dollars if you make a commercial wearing one of our hairpieces on your head."

"Krazlo, over here. I'm Peter Piper from *Weekly* magazine. We've just elected you Man of the Year. Your picture will be on the cover, and I'd like to do a long interview about you."

"Man of the Year? Me? The only award I've ever won was from the Cheese Foundation. They named me Rat of the Month. And now this. I don't know what to say."

"Don't say anything," a man interrupted. "I'm a writer, and I'm going to help you write a book about your life. You'll write about every evil, miserable, sneaky, nasty thing you've ever done. At the end you'll say you're sorry. People will love you."

"Mr. Krazlo, I'd like to make a movie based on your book. I have a contract with me right now." someone else said.

The voices never stopped.

"Mr. Krazlo, would you give a talk at my college?"

"Mr. Krazlo, I'm naming my baby after you. She's bald too."

"Mr. Krazlo, I'd like you to see the Krazlo doll. You see, its eyes turn red and it takes control of all the other dolls."

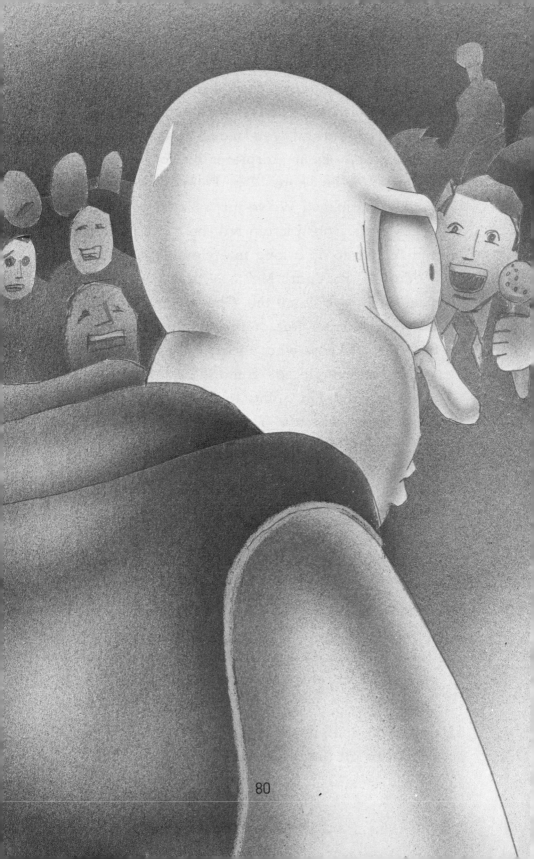

Krazlo sat down. He was dizzy from all this attention. He wished all the noisy people would take their cameras and go. Susan smiled because her plan was working so well.

Then Susan heard the man with the cigar telling Krazlo, "I'm going to make a million dollars. Excuse me, I mean *we* are going to make a million dollars."

Then Susan saw that the sun was coming up.

She ran to the window. It *was* the sun. The whole sun and nothing but the sun! Her superhero friends had saved the Earth.

Susan left to go somewhere quiet. Down in the lobby she turned on the TV. She was listening for news about the sun.

"We'll have an up-to-the-minute report on Krazlo," the announcer said. "We'll know if he slept well, whether he snores, and whether he sleeps with a bald teddy bear —"

Susan tried another station. She saw a bald woman in a cape, saying, "Yes, ladies, think of the money you'll save with the new Krazlo look. You'll never buy shampoo, rollers, or brushes. But you will have to stock up on floor wax —"

Susan flipped the dial again. There was Steve O'Donnell, the weatherman she'd seen before. He too was bald as an egg.

"Well, it looks like it's going to be a beautiful day. So we can all go out and celebrate Krazlo Day in the park. For some reason the cloudy weather has cleared up."

Susan snapped off the television.

No one cares about the sun, Susan thought. They only care about Krazlo. Susan had been trying to get rid of Krazlo, but her plan wasn't working. He was still around. "Maybe people are carrying my plan a little too far," she said.

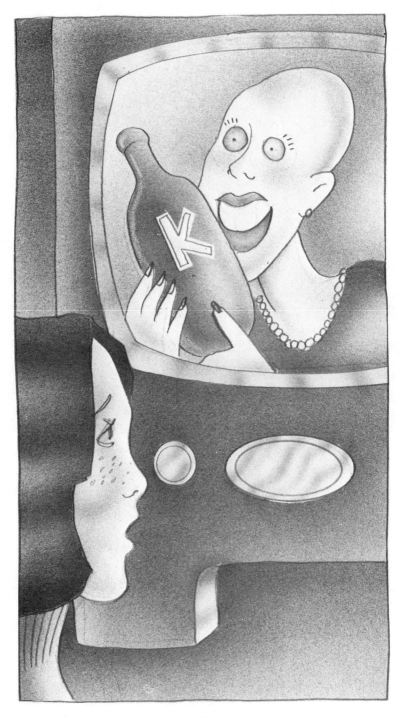

CHAPTER 10

Susan sat in the lobby of the hotel, watching people come in. Everyone asked where Krazlo was and then disappeared into the elevator.

These people have gone Krazlo-crazy and it's my fault, Susan told herself. My plan is a disaster. If only the superheroes would come back.

Susan went to the window to look at the sun. It was beautiful. Then she saw something else, little dots in the sky. They grew larger as they got closer to Earth. And as they got larger, Susan saw the colors of their uniforms—it was the superheroes! They were returning! And they were heading for the hotel!

"Super Susan!" said the Silver Hurricane. "I see you've trapped Krazlo in the hotel. Good work!"

"He's in the hotel," Susan said. "But I wouldn't say I've got him trapped."

Allergyman held up a newspaper. Every headline was about the "wonderful" Krazlo.

"What happened?" asked Silver Hurricane. "Yesterday Krazlo was a villain, and today he's a hero."

"Rock and roll," said Susan.

Susan told the whole story. "So I guess my plan isn't going to work," she said when she finished. "Instead of making Krazlo leave, everyone upstairs is helping him make money."

"Don't worry, Super Susan, we'll take care of him—just like we planned before," said the Silver Hurricane.

But Susan could barely hear him. A strange

noise was coming from outside. It was
drowning out everything. Susan and the
superheroes ran to the windows to see what it
was. Their mouths fell open at the sight.

There were hundreds and hundreds of kids
outside the hotel! They had shaved their heads
and they wore glasses with red lenses. They
were all waiting for America's newest pop star.
They chanted: "We want Krazlo! We want
Krazlo now!"

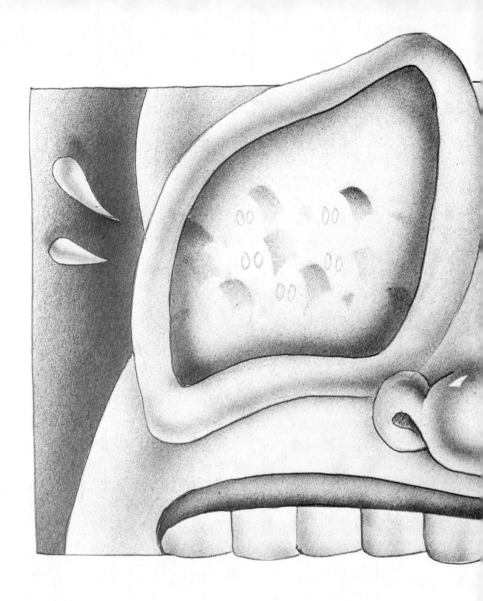

Krazlo stepped out of the hotel elevator. The crowd roared. Krazlo saw them and tried to turn back. He looked scared to death. But he was getting what he deserved.

"Go out there and meet your public," yelled the man with the cigar.

"Uh, how about tomorrow? Maybe I could

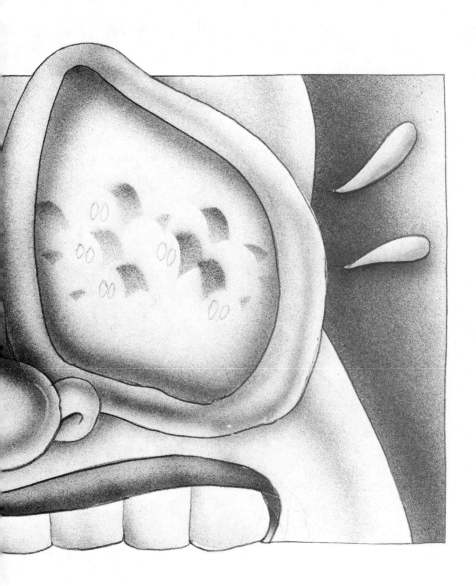

talk to them on the phone instead?"

"Don't be silly. They're your fans. They love you. Let's go," said the man with the cigar. He dragged Krazlo by the arm.

"Do something! Save me! This is all a big mistake!" Krazlo yelled, looking at Susan. But it was too late. He was quickly out the door.

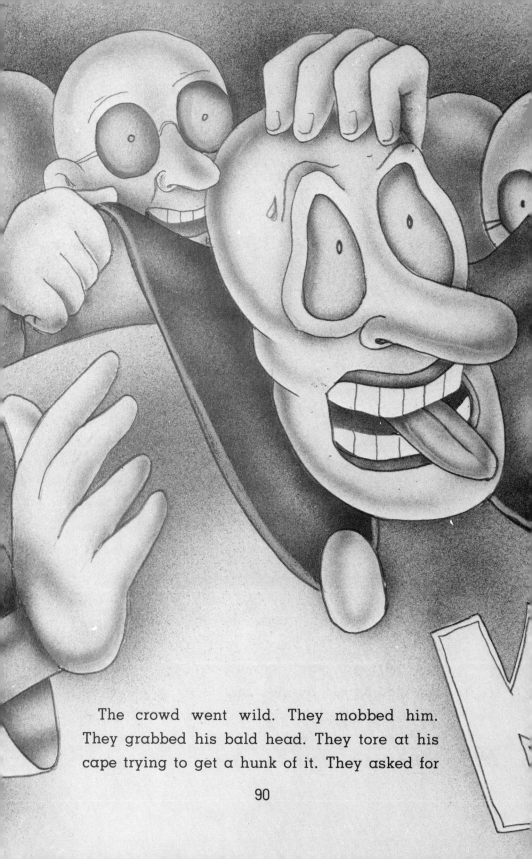

The crowd went wild. They mobbed him.
They grabbed his bald head. They tore at his
cape trying to get a hunk of it. They asked for

his autograph. They demanded a kiss, a bite on the arm—anything. They loved him until he was almost black and blue from the crush.

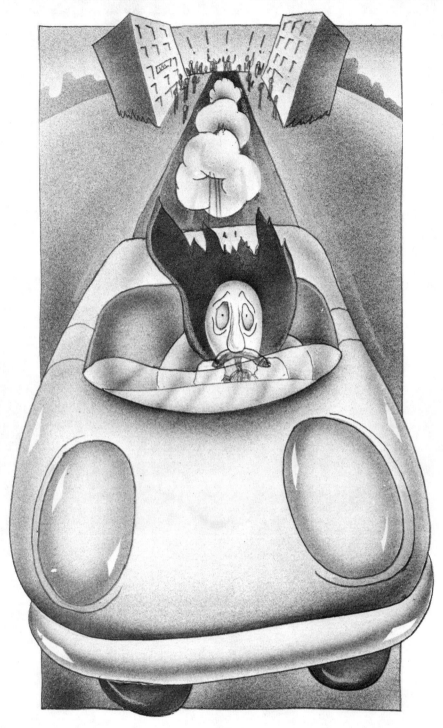

92

Suddenly Krazlo broke away from the crowd and leaped into his car. He drove off at top speed.

Susan could see that Krazlo wasn't planning to come back. Later she saw Krazlo flying away into the sky. All the superheroes smiled and congratulated Susan. Her plan was finally working. Susan smiled, but she sighed with relief, too. Krazlo was finally gone!

"Well, it looks as if our work is finished here," said the Silver Hurricane. "We're needed someplace else. So we'd better get going."

"I can't go with you," Susan said sadly. "I have to see my aunt and uncle in Denver. They're probably very worried about me. I tried to tell you before: I'm not Super Susan. I'm not a superhero. I'm just plain Susan from Fort Wayne, Indiana."

"We knew that," said Worrywoman. "When you didn't fly from the plane or fly with us to the sun, we knew you told us the truth. But you really did help us. Look at all the plans you thought up."

"And you saved Sunburst's life," added Allergyman. "We'll always think of you as Super Susan."

"You'll always be one of us," said the Silver Hurricane. "As for flying, that's easy to arrange."

Worrywoman took one of Susan's hands, and the Silver Hurricane took the other. The three of them flew into the air on a nonstop flight to Denver. The trip went too quickly for Susan. She hated to leave her new friends.

"Good-bye, Super Susan," said the Hurricane. He was gone in a silver gust of wind. Then Worrywoman flew away, too.

Susan watched the sky for a long time after they disappeared. When she turned around, there was her aunt and uncle's house. Susan rushed to the door and rang the bell.

"I'm sorry I made you worry about me, Aunt Edna," Susan said, hugging her aunt and uncle.

"Worry about you? Why should we worry about you?" her aunt asked. "You're a week early!"

"What do you mean, early? I'm a week late!"

"No you're not, dearie," Uncle Bert said. "We weren't expecting you until next week."

"Yes," said Aunt Edna. "Your plans must have gotten fouled up."

When Susan walked into the house, she glanced all around her. There were no newspapers, no magazines. No signs of Krazlo's success at all.

"You don't watch too much television, do you?" Susan asked her aunt.

"That's right, dearie," said her aunt.

Susan thought about all she'd been through. She'd made so many superhero friends: Allergyman, Shyman, Worrywoman, Sunburst, and the Silver Hurricane. Her stomach growled, and it made her think of Hungryman. But Susan would never tell Aunt Edna about her adventures.

Oh, well, Susan told herself. You can't have everything. After all, *I'll* always know that I'm Super Susan, the amazing ten-year-old girl.

She looked up in the sky and smiled. The sun was very, very bright.

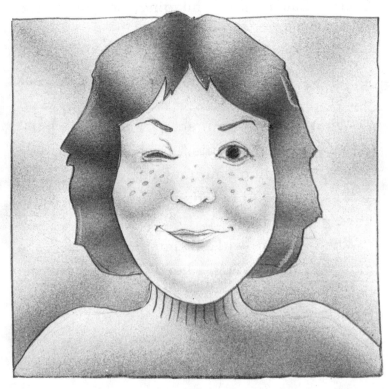